W9-AJP-638

# Mama Travels for Work

Adapted by Jill Cozza-Turner

Based on the screenplay "Jodi's Mama Travels for Work"
written by Leah Gotcsik

Poses and layouts by Jason Fruchter

SCOTT COUNTY LIBRARY SYSTEM

SIMON SPOTLIGHT
An imprint of Simon & Schuster Children's Publishing Division • New York  London  Toronto  Sydney  New Delhi
1230 Avenue of the Americas, New York, New York 10020
This Simon Spotlight paperback edition July 2019
For information about special discounts for bulk purchases, please contact Simon & Schuster Special Sales at
1-866-506-1949 or business@simonandschuster.com. • Manufactured in the United States of America 0619 LAK
1 2 3 4 5 6 7 8 9 10 • ISBN 978-1-5344-4176-7 (pbk) • ISBN 978-1-5344-4177-4 (eBook)

It was a beautiful day in the neighborhood, and Daniel was playing at his neighbor Jodi's house.

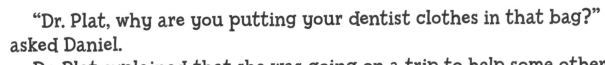

"Dr. Plat, why are you putting your dentist clothes in that bag?" asked Daniel.

Dr. Plat explained that she was going on a trip to help some other children clean their teeth.

"She's going away for three whole days," said Jodi.

"Wow," said Daniel. "Three whole days!"

Jodi hugged her mama. "I'm going to miss you so much!"

"I'm going to miss you, too," said Dr. Plat. "But remember that Nana will be here to take care of you, and you will have your love you loops."

"My love you loops!" said Jodi. Then she sang,

♪ ♫ *"Love you, love you, love you loops!*
*Open a loop every day Mama's away.* ♪
*Love you, love you, love you loops!"*

"What are love you loops?" asked Daniel.

"I have three loops," said Jodi. "I get to open a loop every day at dinnertime, and when I get to the last loop . . . that means Mama is coming home soon!"

"Tigertastic!" said Daniel.

It was time for Dr. Plat to leave, so she gave a big hug to Jodi and her brothers, Teddy and Leo.

Jodi didn't want her mama to leave, but Daniel told Jodi what Mom Tiger always told him when she went to work:

 *"Grown-ups come back!"*

Daniel's mom would come back, and Jodi's mama would come back too.

After Dr. Plat left, Jodi hung her love you loops and sang,

*♪ ♪ "Love you, love you, love you loops! ♪ ♪*
*Open a loop every day Mama's away.*
*Love you, love you, love you loops!"*

Then it was time to play. Daniel and Jodi pretended to be airplanes. "Look!" said Jodi. "I'm flying to work! Zoom! Zoom! But I'll come back!"

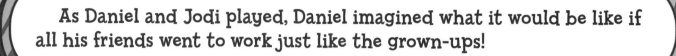
As Daniel and Jodi played, Daniel imagined what it would be like if all his friends went to work just like the grown-ups!

*"Let's go to work like the grown-ups do! Let's go to work, yeah! Me and you!*

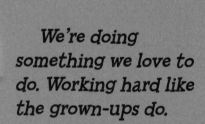

*We're doing something we love to do. Working hard like the grown-ups do.*

Let's go to work like the grown-ups do!

Work real hard, yeah!
Me and you!"

Each day her mama was away, Jodi opened a love you loop and found a surprise from her mama!

The first day, when Jodi opened the first loop, there was a drawing of the cozi-cozi pillow on Jodi's bed. When Jodi went to her bedroom and looked under her pillow, she found sparkly stickers from Mama!

The second day, the love you loop had a picture of the mailbox, and Jodi received a postcard from Mama!

On the third day, there was just one love you loop left. Jodi opened it and saw that it had a picture of a door on it.

"A door? What door?" wondered Daniel.

"Maybe it's *our* door!" said Jodi.

Nana opened the door to Jodi's house, and they saw . . .

. . . Mama! Dr. Plat came back from her trip just like she said she would. Jodi and her brothers were so happy that their mama was home, and their mama was so happy to see them again and hear all about what they had done while she was away!

"Daniel Tiger and I pretended to go to work just like grown-ups!" said Jodi.

"What a great idea!" said Mama.

It wasn't easy for Jodi and her brothers when their mama went away, but now they know:

♪♪♪ *"Grown-ups come back!"* ♪♪

Ugga Mugga!